# The Great Auto Race of 1908

## by Kana Riley

**MODERN CURRICULUM PRESS**

Pearson Learning Group

Back in 1908, riding automobiles was about as rare as riding horses is today. Cars were mostly owned by rich people. They drove them around for fun during the summer. In winter the cars went up on cement blocks in the barn.

You see, back then there were few paved roads. No one had ever heard of a snowplow. And as for antifreeze, it had not been invented yet. The only way to keep your car radiator from freezing during cold weather was to empty out the water.

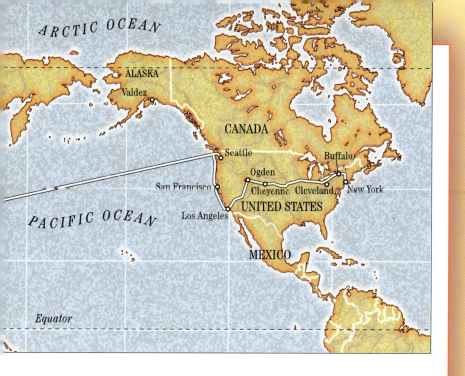

Only a few cars had ever been driven all the way across the United States. The fastest made it in fifteen days. Just one car had traveled round trip. It took ten months! That driver had never tried to travel in bad weather.

But a long tradition in this country is the love of a challenge. So in 1908 two newspapers announced a race. One paper was in Paris, France. The other was in New York City. They would give a prize to the first car to go around the world from New York to Paris — in the winter!

The makers of six cars took up the challenge. Three were from France. The others came from Germany, Italy, and the United States.

The American car was called a Thomas Flyer. Like all of the cars in the race, it was open. It had no top or windshield. At that time people thought it dangerous to have glass in the car. Driver and passengers wore goggles to protect their eyes.

Workers loaded the Thomas. In went gasoline, shovels, axes, chains, ropes, and lanterns. By the time all the cargo was loaded, the car weighed five thousand pounds.

Into it climbed a mechanic named George Schuster, a driver, and a reporter from *The New York Times*. The plan was to head west. They would go most of the way around the world to Paris.

On February 13, 1908, the *Times* reported:
"The six contestants started from Times
Square at 11:15 o'clock yesterday morning. A
throng of fifty thousand persons jammed into
the square."

Flag-waving people "crowded both sides of
Broadway for the eight miles above Times
Square to 200th Street — 150,000 people,
perhaps. The racers and their escort of more
than two hundred automobiles proceeded on
the first stage of their journey."

*Monty Roberts is at the wheel, George Schuster is in the passenger seat, and Walter T. Williams of* The New York Times *rides in back.*

With its brand new forty-five-star American flag flying, the Thomas set off. The goal for the first night was Albany, New York. It was 140 miles away.

The car had not gone far when trouble began. The warm sun had turned the dirt road to mud. Schuster put chains on the tires, but they didn't help much. Time after time, the car got stuck in mud that sometimes reached its hubcaps. Each time the crew had to climb out to shovel the car free.

The engine began to run badly. One of the spark plugs was not firing. Fixing the spark plug meant a stop at a garage. There Schuster made the repairs.

By now it was growing dark. The road ahead was blocked by drifts of snow. The only way to get through was to shovel a path for the car.

Then, while the car was struggling through one of the drifts, its rear end swung around. *Smack!* The car hit a sleigh driven by a local farmer. Dealing with him took up more time.

At last the weary crew pulled into Hudson, New York. It was 8:30 at night. They had traveled only 116 miles in nine hours.

By now it was clear to everyone that this was going to be a very long trip to Paris, France!

It took four days to reach Buffalo, New York. That's where Thomas autos were made. It was also George Schuster's hometown.

He and his crew waved good-by to friends and family. Between them and San Francisco, California, lay more than three thousand miles of winter weather.

One night a blizzard piled snow so deep it nearly covered the car. A farmer opened his house to the crew. After feeding them fresh doughnuts and hot coffee in front of a crackling fire, he offered to help. He hitched up his team of horses and broke a path for the car. It took until mid-morning to reach the town. They had traveled seven miles in twelve hours.

Despite the hardships, the crew did have fun. One night in Rawlins, Wyoming, local folks put on a seven-course banquet to honor the racers. There were souvenirs and special dishes for the event.

But soon they were on the road again. Sometimes they followed railroad tracks. Sometimes they hired guides. Through deserts and mountains, the Thomas Flyer kept going.

At last, on March 24, the American car pulled into San Francisco. One French car had dropped out. The others were far behind. The Flyer changed crew, and George Schuster took a turn as the driver.

The planned route for the race ran across Alaska. From there the cars were supposed to drive on the ice over the Bering Strait to Siberia.

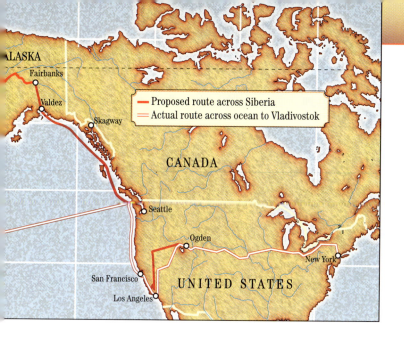

ALASKA
Fairbanks
Valdez
Skagway

CANADA

Seattle

Ogden
New York

San Francisco
Los Angeles
UNITED STATES

— Proposed route across Siberia
═ Actual route across ocean to Vladivostok

After a few days' rest, Schuster and his crew loaded the Thomas onto a boat. They set sail for Valdez, Alaska. A lively crowd greeted them there. And no wonder! The Flyer was the first car anyone in that town had ever seen.

It was also the last for a while. The snow was so deep, Schuster couldn't drive the car off the dock.

Quickly he sent a telegram to the race planners. The next day he got a reply: ROUTE CHANGED . . . GO TO SEATTLE and then TO VLADIVOSTOK (Vlad-a-VOS-tock).

While the Thomas was still in Alaska, the four other cars sailed across the Pacific. Race organizers told them all to wait at Vladivostok, Russia. That way all the cars would start again at the same time.

In addition, the German car was penalized thirty days. Back in the United States, it had bogged down hopelessly in Idaho. So its drivers had loaded the car onto a train. They rode to Seattle by rail. Now to win, the German car would have to get to Paris thirty days before the Americans.

On May 18, the Thomas and the others prepared to leave Vladivostok. The Siberian city was gloomy with rain. A Russian looked at the cars loaded with gear for the trip. "This is madness," he said. "You will never get through."

Schuster would recall those words often as he and the crew slogged through mud, battled clouds of gnats, and forded swollen rivers.

His car felt the strain too. Tires burst. The frame broke. Gears were stripped. While traveling across America, Schuster and crew could stop at garages for parts. In Russia, there was no such help. Once, to repair a gear, they had to make new teeth for it at a village blacksmith shop.

Another time, Schuster was driving into a Russian village. Ahead, a dozen chickens were in the road. He waited for the mechanic to blow the horn. Closer and closer he came to the birds. Then he looked over. His mechanic was fast asleep with the horn held tightly in his hands. The feathers flew that day!

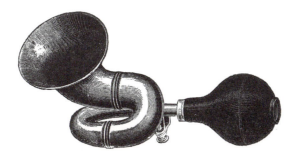

Spring turned into summer. Only two cars were left in the running, the German and the American ones. Even though Schuster and his crew had been given a thirty-day lead, they did not slack off. During the seventy-two day crossing of Siberia they stopped to sleep only five times. All through the race, the lead went back and forth.

At last, on July 26, the German car chugged into Paris. Only four days behind it came the Thomas. Because of the penalty, it had won!

As the Thomas neared Paris, it picked up speed. Soon it was rattling along at fifty miles an hour over cobblestone roads.

Word of its arrival began to spread. Crowds gathered along the road. Bicyclists rode alongside.

"Long live the American auto!"people called.
Into Paris rolled the Thomas Flyer. It had
traveled 13,341 miles.

The first thing George Schuster did was get
a good night's sleep. Then he picked up some
souvenirs for his family and boarded a ship
for home.

Back in the United States, Schuster and his crew met President Theodore Roosevelt. Afterward they liked to recall Roosevelt's words. "I admire," said the president, "Americans who do things, whether it is going up in a balloon, or down in a submarine, or driving an automobile around the world."

Today the Thomas Flyer has been restored. It sits in the National Auto Museum in Reno, Nevada. There it reminds us of the long tradition of hardy folks who overcame great obstacles to win.